Stinky Cynthia

Stinky Cynthia

HEATHER EYLES

Illustrated by Tony Ross

RED FOX

A Red Fox Book

Published by Random House Children's Books
20 Vauxhall Bridge Road, London SW1V 2SA

A division of Random House UK Ltd
London Melbourne Sydney Auckland
Johannesburg and agencies throughout the world

1 3 5 7 9 10 8 6 4 2

First published simultaneously in hardback and paperback by
The Bodley Head Children's Books and Red Fox 1995

Set in 12/26pt Plantin
Printed and bound in Great Britain by
Cox and Wyman Ltd, Reading, Berkshire
RANDOM HOUSE UK Limited Reg. No. 954009

ISBN 0 09 9371316

This is a story about someone no one will love. In fact, this is a story about someone absolutely no one will even like. Unless . . .

This is a story about a rat.

Not just any old rat, but a horrible, dirty, stinky, revolting rat called Cynthia.

Cynthia lived in a sewer. That means she lived down a drain. There were lots of rats living in the sewer, all of them horrible, dirty and revolting, but Cynthia was the stinkiest of them all!

Even the other rats thought so.

'Phew!' they would squeak when Cynthia ran past. 'There goes stinky Cynthia!'

Cynthia had no rat friends at all and even the crawly, squirmy things that lived down the drain and the spiders wouldn't speak to her. She was just too absolutely revolting for words. Her mother had been caught by a cat when she was quite, quite small, up in the big, wide world, and Cynthia had never learnt how to keep herself clean. Nor did she ever dare go 'upstairs', in case the same thing happened to her.

Deep, deep down in the darkest, coldest, smelliest part of the sewer the rats had a special meeting place, a Rat Parliament, where they would meet and discuss really important things, like which local café had the most overflowing dustbins. They often served refreshments of the finest mouldy cheese and rotten bananas, but Cynthia was never invited to any of these meetings. All she got to eat was leftover leftovers when all the other rats had eaten themselves fit to bursting.

Poor Cynthia got thinner and thinner.

And smellier and smellier.

Sometimes Cynthia would sit under the grating of the drain and look up at the light through the bars. She could see the feet and legs of humans as they scurried past on their way to work. One or two of them she could recognize by their footsteps as they came past every day.

There was a little girl who walked with a skip and a hop down the street and who always stopped to peer through the grating into the deep, dark drain. Cynthia kept very still so as not to scare her.

Then there was an old man who shuffled along banging his stick on the pavement. He was always muttering to himself, which frightened Cynthia, until she realized he couldn't reach down into her dark, dirty world.

Then there were the young mothers with their babies in pushchairs, bumping over the kerb. The babies often dropped their biscuits or their crisps and the food would fall between the bars, down the drain and straight into

5

Cynthia's waiting mouth. Once a whole ice-cream cornet landed upside down on the grating and dripped for hours onto Cynthia's outstretched tongue!

Oh how she wished she was up there in the sunlight, even if she had no one to talk to. Anything would be better than living with nasty rats that bared their teeth whenever she came near and snarled at her.

'Stinky Cynthia! What a pong!'

So Cynthia just kept out of everybody's way under the grating and dreamed and dreamed . . . until . . .

One day the rains came.

First the air grew heavy and sticky and down in the

sewer the rats could smell the thunder in the air and became very excited and squeaky. They scurried about bumping into each other and falling over themselves trying to find the best and safest ledges to sit on, so they wouldn't get wet when the storm broke and the rain came pouring down the drain.

'Out of my way!' they shouted at Cynthia. 'I'm not sitting with you! Get off my ledge! This is my ledge! We don't want you here! Oh, what a pong!'

So Cynthia just went and sat under the grating as usual, staring up into the darkening sky. She wanted to feel the rain pattering onto her fur.

Perhaps it will wash some of the smell off, she thought.

The air was thick and heavy. The light above the grating was hardly any brighter than the gloom in the sewer. It seemed as if the whole world was waiting for something to happen. She could hear feet running quickly

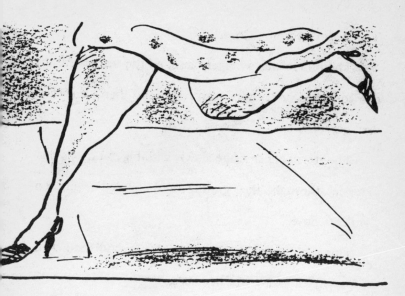

by on the pavement above.

'We're in for a big one,' she heard someone say.

'It's as dark as night,' said another. 'Better get indoors.'

Far off in the distance, Cynthia heard a booming, growling sound. It set all the rats squeaking and rushing about, pushing each other off the narrow ledges and out of the nooks and crannies they had hidden in for safety.

'Thunder!' she heard them saying. 'It's the thunder!

The storm's coming closer!'

Then there was a bigger bang, a little nearer. All the rats squeaked once more with fright and then went very, very quiet.

The storm began quite slowly with big, fat drops that plopped through the grating and landed right on Cynthia's nose.

This is nice, she thought, free drink! And she licked the lovely clean water off her nose.

Suddenly, there was a great sizzling sound and the whole world lit up in a white flash that was brighter than the sun. It was followed almost at once by an enormous bang that shook the whole sewer and some of the rats fell off their perching places. Cynthia could hear them splashing into the water and grumbling as they swam back to dry land. Bigger and bigger drops plopped through the grating. Cynthia heard one last human run across the road and disappear into their front door with a loud clunk.

Then, as if the whole world was giving a sigh, the rain really began.

Drops, fatter and fatter, faster and faster, came pattering down the drain, soaking Cynthia right through to her skin. Still she sat there, not wanting to join the other rats jostling for a dry space in the dark. Nobody would give her an inch anyway. She'd rather get wet and make herself all nice and clean in this lovely shower from the sky.

But the water began to stream through the drain, first in a trickle, then in a waterfall, then in a torrent as the storm finally broke and the rain swept down the roads in rivers and disappeared down the drains like the Niagara Falls.

As the water hit Cynthia, she lost her grip on the side of the drain. She scratched helplessly with her claws at the concrete and tried to hold on, but the force of the water took her breath away. Before she knew it, she was swept and whirled off into the deep cavern of the sewer.

The rush and roar of the water boomed in Cynthia's ears as she was scraped against the walls of the sewer.

Endless, endless tunnels. Dark as night.

Crash! She hit the wall of one bend. Bang! She bumped into a jutting out ledge.

She tried to swim, her paws fighting against the great wall of water, but it was hopeless. The force was too strong for her, too fast and too heavy. It was easiest and best just to give in to the great roaring river. So she let it carry her on and on, holding her up, bumping her round corners and all the time sounding like thunder in her ears.

After a long nightmare during which she felt that every bit of fur must have been scraped from her body, Cynthia at last saw grey light approaching. Gradually it became brighter and brighter and suddenly Cynthia was swept out of the tunnel in a great waterfall and she landed – plop – in something dark and cold and very, very deep.

Cynthia began to swim for dear life. She didn't even know which way was up, but she headed for the part of this dark, murky substance that looked a bit lighter than the rest. With her limbs aching and her lungs ready to burst, at last her head broke above water!

Above her, instead of the bricks and concrete of the sewer, or the rungs of the grating, was this enormous space, a mixture of blues and reds with clouds drifting across it. Cynthia had only ever seen the sky through the grating of the drain before but, as she floated on her back in the murky cold water, she thought the silvery edges to the clouds looked so beautiful against the multi-coloured sky that, for a moment, she forgot to swim for the shore.

Then, even in her exhausted state, she realized she must find land. She moved her back legs and feebly paddled with her front paws and slowly she began to drift through the water. A gentle current was carrying her downstream but, as she moved her bruised body, she began to make some progress towards the shore.

Just when she felt she couldn't keep going any longer, a transparent shape like a ghostly silver coin swam out from behind the clouds and floated across the sky.

That must be the moon, thought Cynthia. Why

17

didn't anyone tell me how beautiful it is! Maybe I've died
and gone to Rat Heaven.

That was the last thing Cynthia was aware of until
she woke up with a stone under her head and the tempting
smell of rotting rubbish not far away. She twitched her
nose and moved her paws. She had not gone to heaven
after all. She was still here and she was cold and hungry.

It was night. The street lamps high above on the

embankment were lit, but down below by the water all was in damp darkness. Cynthia staggered as she got up. Every bit of her seemed to be sore and aching from all those bumps in the sewer.

The sewer! How far away it seemed now! Here there was all this space under a sky that was now black and, away from the glare of the street lights, was studded with tiny, gleaming stars. But, first things first! There wasn't

time to admire the scenery. Cynthia could smell food!

She burrowed her nose into the pile of rotting vegetation that had been washed up by the river against the steps. There were apples and oranges, bananas and melons, a little rotten and slimy with a few maggots, but Cynthia didn't care, it was bliss! She ate until her stomach could take no more. Then, almost groaning with the weight of her feast, she was just turning away when she caught sight of another rat on the other side of the heap.

What a beautiful creature! thought Cynthia, but she won't speak to me. She's so glamorous, with such lovely fluffy fur, and here am I so stinky and dirty and ugly.

But the rat did not go away, rather it looked harder at Cynthia and as Cynthia moved gingerly towards her, the rat made a move as if she too wanted to be friendly. Slowly, slowly, Cynthia made her way towards the gorgeous creature and it was only when their noses were almost touching that Cynthia jumped in surprise. She suddenly realized it was her own reflection in a broken

piece of mirrored glass that had been washed up with the pile of fruit. But where were the ugly matted, dark fur and the dirt? This beautiful creature gleamed and shone and her face was framed in a halo of fluffy fur.

Then she remembered the water and the bumpings and the thumpings and the scouring her fur had received in the tunnel and she looked again and saw what a clean, lovely creature she had become.

Carefully, Cynthia cleaned her whiskers of the last remaining bits of squashed fruit, thinking hard. A little bit of dangerous pride began to creep into her ratty mind.

A gorgeous creature like her should be out in the world, showing herself off to other rats. Wasn't that right? She was as good as any of them now. She could do anything. She scurried to the bottom of the stone steps and looked up into the street lights. That was where she belonged, up there in the great wide world. Now she would show them!

At the top of the stone steps, the beautiful, glittering world she had glimpsed from the river bank suddenly turned into a horrible, roaring, rushing, honking, smelly, smoky hell. Huge metal things with big, rubber feet rushed at her as she tried to cross the road. Cynthia shrank trembling into the gutter, feeling very frightened and very, very alone.

As she crouched for a few moments by a drain, looking down at the old world she knew so well, a huge, red, smoke-breathing metal monster with a loud roar came out of nowhere and almost squashed her flat with its rolling foot. Cynthia jumped into the air with a loud squeal and ran blindly into the traffic, weaving this way and that, wheels brushing her whiskers and almost squashing her tail.

At last she made it over to the opposite pavement. She slunk along the wall, away from the passing feet, and gratefully slid into the first dark alleyway she could find. There she hid behind two smelly dustbins, shaking all over from fright.

'Oh!' she cried, 'I wish I was back home in the sewer. There weren't giants there to roar at me and squash me flat!'

But after a few minutes, Cynthia began to calm down and look around her. She looked at the dustbins overflowing with delicious, rotting food.

At least I'm not hungry, she thought. I was always hungry down in the sewer. Up here in the world there's plenty of food, all for me. It's put here just for me to eat.

Just then a face with beady eyes and whiskers appeared from behind one of the dustbins. The rest of its body followed. It was a HUGE rat, its body rippling with glistening muscles.

'Hey you!' it sneered at her. 'Yeah you! You over there! Are you deaf? What do you think you're doing 'ere, eh? This is my patch. Clear off!'

'Your patch?' whispered Cynthia in a very high, nervous squeak. 'I don't know what you mean.'

'I'll show you what I mean,' threatened the huge rat and he leapt at her, his teeth bared and snarling.

Cynthia did not try to stop and fight. Instead, she turned round and, as quick as a flash, slipped away into the darkness of the alley. But not before she felt the sharp nip of teeth on the very end of her tail. When she had reached safety she turned to see what had happened. The tip of her tail had gone! Vanished! Disappeared for ever into the jaws of the huge rat!

Cynthia put the end of her wounded tail into her mouth to lick it better. I think, thought Cynthia, I think, all things considered, I don't like it here very much. I think I'd rather be back with the nasty old rats being horrible to me and not talking to me. At least they didn't bite my tail off!

But it was only a thought and Cynthia did not have it for long. She was too busy trying to find shelter from the rapidly growing daylight, the increasing danger of millions of feet pounding and tramping the pavements and the roaring of metal monsters.

At last, in a doorway, she came across just the very thing: an old plastic bag filled with all sorts of rubbish to make a bed in – old socks, scarves, gloves, even a fur hat. Best of all, nestling inside all this warm softness was a lovely, stale cake with icing sugar on the top and currants inside.

As Cynthia settled down to sleep inside the fur hat with soft, woolly socks on top of her and with a deliciously full stomach, she thought to herself: This is the life. This is paradise. And I'm oh-so-sleepy after my long journey. I could just sleep for ever and ever ... and ...

She woke to find her nice warm bed bumping and swaying about which made her stomach feel funny. It bumped down with a jolt and then it was up again, gently swinging around, tipping first one way then another.

Cynthia put her nose out of her nice warm bed and looked over the edge of the bag. There was the pavement way beneath her, swaying about, and there right above her was a large, knobbly, dirty human hand holding on to the straps of the bag. Higher up was a grey woolly coat with string tied around the waist and higher even than that, almost as high as the sky it seemed to Cynthia, was a round, red, human face with bumps all over it and highest of all was a brown woolly hat pulled down around the face's ears.

Cynthia's first thought was to jump out and run away, but she looked down at the pavement swaying about beneath her and it looked too far to jump.

Instead, she burrowed right back down to the bottom of the bag as far as she could go and hid there, not knowing what on earth was going to happen, her nose pressed right up against some very squashed sandwiches and a wrinkled old apple. She was much too frightened

33

even to think about taking a nibble out of them.

The next time the bag stops moving about, I'm off, she thought and lay very, very still.

At last she felt the bag go down with a plonk. She was just getting ready to make a jump for it when she felt the weight of the clothes above her beginning to get lighter and lighter. Then daylight appeared and a hand stretched down into the bag.

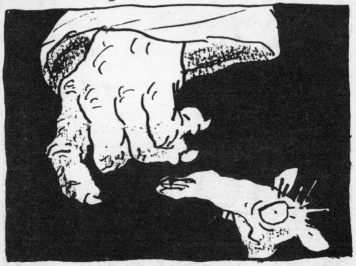

'Where are those old sandwiches of mine. Just fancy a cheese and pickle,' she heard the human muttering. As

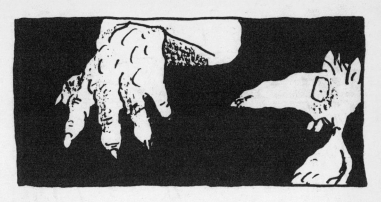

the hand began to feel around in the bottom of the bag,
Cynthia crouched in the corner, her heart beating so
loudly in her ears she thought she was going to faint. The
hand groped about, first grasping the apple and letting it
go and then going into one corner as it felt for the
sandwiches. Then, horror of horrors, it closed around

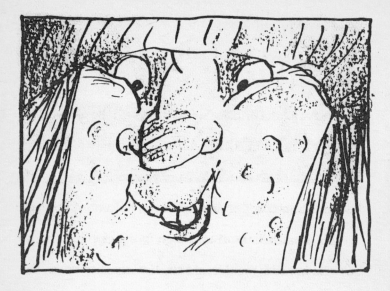

her! She was trapped in the huge red hand! Too frightened

to bite, or even wriggle out of danger, Cynthia blinked as

she was drawn out into the bright sunshine and found

herself staring into a pair of bright, twinkling eyes with

millions of little furrows around them.

'Well, well, what have we here? This is a funny kind

of sandwich. What are you, my dear? I can't see very well

these days. Are you a kitten? A sweet little kitten who's

lost its mother? How did you end up in my bag, dearie?'

I'm not a kitten, thought Cynthia, but don't tell anyone! I'm a rat, a rat, nobody likes rats. She thinks I'm a kitten. Oh please!

'Have a little drink of milk, kitty,' said the old woman. 'I've got a bit of milk here for you.' She poured the milk from a battered carton into an old yogurt pot and gave it to Cynthia to drink on her lap.

As Cynthia lapped up the milk, the old lady stroked her with her finger and hummed. 'Lovely kitty, lovely soft

fur, so soft and fine, so pretty. You're pretty kitty, little kitty.'

Just then another human, equally large and shapeless and dressed in ragged, old clothes, came and sat next to the old woman on the bench.

'Hallo there, Cyn,' he said.

Cynthia pricked up her ears. Was he talking to her? How did he know her name? 'What you got there then, Cyn?'

'A pretty kitty,' said the old woman. 'A lovely pretty kitty to keep me company.'

The other human bent down closer to the old woman's lap and peered at Cynthia. She could see the bristles on his chin and his teeth all yellowed and chipped.

'That ain't no kitty, Cyn,' he said. 'Ho, ho! That ain't no kitty. That there, what you've got there, that be a rat. That's what that be. A blooming rat!'

The old lady stopped stroking Cynthia and looked down at her. She brought her eyes very close to Cynthia's and peered at her. Cynthia kept so still that her heart almost stopped beating.

Then the woman sat back. 'Well I'll be . . .!' she said. 'Well I never . . .!'

Then she began to laugh. She laughed and she laughed and she laughed so much she had to hold her sides and tears ran down her round and lumpy cheeks. 'Well I'll be . . .!'

When she had almost finished laughing she said to the man, 'Well, she don't bite!' and it set her off laughing some more.

'Oh dearie,' she said at last. 'I haven't laughed so much in twenty years. Not since I set out on the road. Me sitting here with a rat on my lap, as calm as you like – a rat.'

'Nasty, smelly, dirty things,' said the man, poking at Cynthia with a filthy fingernail and a hand so black with dirt it had engrained itself into the skin. 'You have to watch out, they carry diseases, they do. Kill it, that's what you should do.'

41

Then he lifted Cynthia up by her poor wounded tail and swung her about. 'I'll drown her for you,' he said.

'Oi!' said the old woman, grabbing her back. 'She's not dirty, are you love? Or no dirtier than I am meself. I reckon you and me don't get too many baths, eh? But you seem clean enough to me. I like the look of you, rat or no rat. You gave me the best laugh I've had in years and you can't say fairer than that.'

That night Cynthia slept snuggled up inside the grey woolly coat tied up with string. And so the two Cynthias kept each other company through the night.

Cynthia didn't get too many baths after that day. In fact, she did not get any at all and as time wore on she got dirtier and dirtier until she looked quite like her old self. Well, not quite as bad. But it did not seem to matter very much.

She and the old woman scavenged the dustbins for food and they both became as grimy as each other. So if anyone in the street called out 'Hey! Stinky Cynthia!', they did not know which one of them was being called names. And, to be honest, they did not really care.

In fact, the two of them became quite famous and before long shopkeepers and café owners were keeping special bits of food for them, the old woman and her rat, the two Stinky Cynthias.

Just sometimes, Cynthia would go and stand over a drain and look down into the dark world she had left behind and wonder what her own kind were doing down there and she longed, just for a minute, for some rat-talk.

But most of the time she was happy to be where she was with her best friend Cynthia. She knew she was free to come and go through the streets as she pleased. And that any night she could snuggle up under the grey woolly coat tied up with string and keep her friend warm.